Davyology

PRAISE FOR *STORYSHARES*

"One of the brightest innovators and game-changers in the education industry."
– Forbes

"Your success in applying research-validated practices to promote literacy serves as a valuable model for other organizations seeking to create evidence-based literacy programs."

- Library of Congress

"We need powerful social and educational innovation, and Storyshares is breaking new ground. The organization addresses critical problems facing our students and teachers. I am excited about the strategies it brings to the collective work of making sure every student has an equal chance in life."
– Teach For America

"Around the world, this is one of the up-and-coming trailblazers changing the landscape of literacy and education."
- International Literacy Association

"It's the perfect idea. There's really nothing like this. I mean wow, this will be a wonderful experience for young people." - Andrea Davis Pinkney, Executive Director, Scholastic

"Reading for meaning opens opportunities for a lifetime of learning. Providing emerging readers with engaging texts that are designed to offer both challenges and support for each individual will improve their lives for years to come. Storyshares is a wonderful start."
- David Rose, Co-founder of CAST & UDL

Davyology

Craig Merrow

STORYSHARES

Story Share, Inc.
New York. Boston. Philadelphia

Published in the United States by Story Share, Inc.

Storyshares
Story Share, Inc.
24 N. Bryn Mawr Avenue #340
Bryn Mawr, PA 19010-3304
www.storyshares.org

Inspiring reading with a new kind of book.

Interest Level: High School
Grade Level Equivalent: 4.2

9781973489801

Book design by Storyshares

Printed in the United States of America

Storyshares Presents

1

Karen was enjoying dinner with Joshua and his parents when a loud slam interrupted them. Everyone turned to see Davy explode through the kitchen door, ranting and raving as he grabbed a box of ice cream from the freezer and made himself at home at the dinner table.

"Geez, what a racket they have going! I didn't even have any say in it. What kind of school are they running, anyways? Someone is going to hear about this!"

"Why, what happened?" asked Karen.

Davy began to scoop ice cream with a spoon and cram it in his mouth. “That stupid guidance counselor I have put me into a class that I never signed up for. I swear that woman is the Anti-Christ or something. She really makes me mad!”

“Why, what’s that class?” asked Joshua.

Davy reached across the table and grabbed a biscuit. “Psychology,” he said with considerable disgust before stuffing the biscuit in his mouth.

“Psychology isn't so bad,” interjected Joshua's mother. “It's actually a very interesting subject. What's wrong with that?”

“That rotten Mrs. Quackenbush signed me up without even asking me, and she won't let me drop it, either!” he grunted as he shoveled another spoonful of ice cream into his mouth. “She claimed it would be 'good for me,'” he added, holding up his fingers as quotation marks to emphasize the point.

“That would be an understatement,” said Joshua's father.

“Oh yeah?” Davy shot back. “What does she know? Why do I need psychology? I'm fine! There's nothing wrong with me!" he exclaimed, reaching across the table and grabbing Karen's glass. He chugged down its contents in one shot. Then he got up from the table, bumping it and rattling everything on it. "Boy, has she got some nerve," he added as he left the table.

He stopped and tossed the empty box back in the freezer, calling back, "Oh, by the way, you're out of ice cream again!" before slamming the kitchen door shut behind him, shaking the whole house as he did so.

Joshua's mother and father looked at each other in puzzlement. Joshua glanced over at Karen, who was peering into her empty glass.

"So what do you think?" he asked.

"Going to be a really interesting semester," she replied.

2

"What happened to this one?" asked Joshua, surveying Davy's latest set of wheels.

"I don't know, except it's so bad, I can't even tell you what it used to be," replied Davy, running his fingers along what remained of the rusty, demolished bodywork that was covered in graffiti.

"It's a really ugly car, too," added Joshua. "This is the first Batmobile you've had that looks the part."

"Yeah," agreed Davy. "It's a face only a mother could love."

Davy cranked the starter a few times before the wreck rattled to life. Joshua observed the outside mirror shaking around on its mount as he commented, "This is definitely one of the roughest cars you've had."

"Yeah, but it was the only thing available, so I had to take what I could get," Davy replied as the transmission gave a sickening crunch.

"Provided it gets us there," Joshua pointed out, matter-of-factly.

Davy just shrugged. "Yeah, but one can always hope," he added as he pulled up in Karen's driveway.

They didn't even get out of the car before Karen bounded out the front door. She stopped in her tracks to laugh at the car Davy was driving. Then she yanked open the back door and hopped inside.

"Geez, Davy, this thing is really screwed up! Where did you find such an ugly car?" she giggled.

"The Screw-Up Fairy beat it with an ugly stick," scolded Davy with his face all contorted in a mocking frown. “Besides, it's not THAT bad! This car is ME! It fits me like a fine leather glove.”

Karen surveyed the interior. “Your leather glove has springs poking up through the seat.”

“Yeah, well, poke it back!”

“Boy, you sure are testy this morning. Aren't you excited about your classes?”

Davy dropped it in reverse with a loud grinding sound and backed out of the driveway. “No.”

“Not looking forward to Psychology?” asked Joshua.

“No,” came the flat reply as Davy ground it into drive.

Karen bounced on the back seat. “Why not? That sounds like an interesting class!”

“That's because you're not the one taking it.”

“What's wrong with Psychology?” asked Karen.

“I got Roger Fredericks, that's what.”

“And what's wrong with him?” asked Joshua.

“He's the inverse of Fred Rogers,” grunted Davy. “And he's old, too... almost as old as my Aunt Vera. And worst of all, he's the ONLY one who teaches it!”

“You need to keep an open mind,” countered Karen. “Think of all the great things you'll learn from that class, like how and why people act the way they do.”

Then Joshua said the wrong thing: “At the very least, Davy, try to have some fun with it.”

Joshua popped open the glove box to see what was inside. Neither Josh nor Karen noticed the look of evil genius that had crept across Davy's face or realized what they had unintentionally started.

3

"So how did everything go today?" asked Joshua as they walked into the parking lot at the end of the day.

Karen shifted her load of textbooks before answering. "Not too bad. It's always a little overwhelming on the first day of class, but Political Science and World Affairs are really interesting subjects. How was yours?"

"Pretty good. It worked out so that I have Finance and Economics back-to-back. Each class has information that ties into the other, so there's going to be some interesting overlap."

As they approached the car, Karen looked around. "Where's Davy? He's usually the first one out of the gate."

"He told me he would be a few minutes," said Joshua as he opened the back door for Karen. "Something about going to the library."

Karen was surprised. "Davy went to the library? That's a first... I didn't think he even knew we had one."

"Well, we'll find out soon. Here he comes!"

Davy walked up to the car with something in his hand. Karen rolled down the window and called out, "Did you actually check something out from the library?"

Davy opened the door and hopped in. "Not quite, Cupcake," he answered, handing her a notebook.

Karen took it and leafed through the blank pages. "Well, it's a start. Planning to actually take notes in class?"

"I thought he was going to use it for drawing flip-book, animated cartoons," said Joshua.

"No, I wouldn't use it for that," replied Davy. = "That's what my textbooks are for."

Karen tossed the notebook over the seat, where it plopped down next to Davy. "So what are you going to use it for?" she asked.

"Psychology," stated Davy rather flatly.

Joshua raised his eyebrows. "You're actually going to take notes in Psychology? I thought you didn't want anything to do with that class. How did it go today?"

"It was OK," said Davy as he started the car and backed it out of the parking space.

"That's it? Just OK? Tell us more," prodded Karen.

"Well," said Davy, dropping the car into drive with a crunch. "Mr. Fredericks gave us our textbook, our course outline, and what to expect..."

"Where is your textbook?" asked Joshua.

"In my locker," replied Davy. "Anyways, he told us that he wanted us to take notes on things that happen around us and how people react in a given situation. As the class progresses, we will look at our notes and learn how to analyze and understand the things we recorded. Then we will write a report on our findings. After that, he went around the room and asked what kind of first impressions we get when we meet someone for the first time, such as himself."

"What kind of answer did you give?" asked Karen, looking up from one of her textbooks.

"I told him he looked like someone who wears starched underwear."

Joshua and Karen gave each other a puzzled look. "Well," said Joshua slowly. "Ask a stupid question..."

Davy looked at him and beamed.

4

Davy, Joshua, and Karen studied quietly in the kitchen.

It was Joshua who finally broke the silence. "How's it going?" he asked, looking up from his laptop and textbooks that were spread across one end of the kitchen table.

Karen was at the other end of the table with her laptop and a stack of magazines, notebooks, and textbooks around her.

"Um, OK, I guess," she sighed, rubbing her eyes. "This is some pretty intense stuff." Then she glanced over to where Davy was reading on the kitchen floor. "Hey, Batman, how's everything down there?"

Davy swallowed another spoonful of ice cream. "Not so good," came the reply. "The Joker pulled a fast one."

"I thought you were studying for Psychology?" asked Joshua.

"I was. Then I finished."

"Where's your textbook?"

"In my locker."

Karen scribbled a couple of notes. "So how did your class go today?" she asked, leaning back in her chair to stretch.

"Well, we had to look at a situation and compare how different people deal with it."

"That's interesting," said Joshua. "What situation did you examine?"

"The Brady Bunch and the Hollywood Squares."

"What does that have to do with Psychology?" asked Karen.

Davy turned the page of his comic book. "Everything! For starters, they're both stuck in those little boxes," he explained. "What I want to know is how they got in there, and how do they get out? What did they do to get in there? Why are they still there? Are they being punished? And if they are, why do they look so happy?"

Karen puzzled over this for a moment. "That's really not much of a report."

"I'll say... I had more questions than answers," Davy said. "Fredericks had a few questions about it, too."

"Like what?" asked Joshua.

"Oh, some irrelevant stuff, like what was I thinking, what do I expect to get out of the class, was just messing with him... Oh, that reminds me." Davy picked up his notebook and scribbled a few things in it before getting up and tossing the empty ice cream box back in the freezer.

"Hey, Karen," Davy said. "Tell your Mom to buy the ice cream with the marshmallow bits in it next time."

5

“This class sucks,” Davy complained during lunch period. “I don't think Fredericks likes me.”

“Why, what did you do this time?” asked Karen. She nibbled on a piece of celery as she read her textbook.

“I didn't do anything!” he replied as he snarfed potato chips from a bag.

Joshua thought for a moment, swirling his container of juice around. “Actually, that's not far from the truth. You really haven't done much of anything in that class since you started."

"That isn't true!" Davy retorted through a mouthful of chips. "I've done all my assignments!"

"Sort of," added Karen. "But you haven't put much effort into them."

"Hey, hey, hey," Davy scolded. "It just so happens that I put a LOT of effort into my latest assignment."

"Really? What did he assign you this time?" asked Karen in a rather ominous tone.

"Well, we had to draw a parallel between two different cultures in similar environments and analyze how they fared in a given situation."

"So what did you do analyze?" asked Joshua.

"I compared The Wizard of Oz to The Wizard of Id, and...

Karen went into a fit of uncontrollable laughter when she heard this. Joshua buried his face in his hands to maintain some composure. Everyone in the cafeteria looked in their direction to see what all the noise was about.

Davy hollered over the din at Karen. “It's not THAT funny!” he exclaimed. “Think about it – one is run by a phony, the other by a fink. Both the peasants and Munchkins are suppressed, but one has Judy Garland to rescue them. The peasants have nobody, and...”

Karen was laughing so hard she had tears streaming from her eyes. She probably didn't even hear Davy. But Joshua did, and although he tried, he couldn't quite keep his composure either.

“Geez, what did Mr. Fredericks have to say about that?”

“He didn't say much... He was too busy trying to get his aspirin bottle open,” Davy added as he opened his notebook and started writing.

6

Joshua's parents were out for the evening, so the house appeared empty when he got home. He plopped his books down on the kitchen counter, then opened the freezer for some ice cream. He started to pull the box out, then paused. He opened the lid and peered inside to find it empty. He closed the freezer, put the empty box in the recycling bin, and called out, "What's up, Batman?"

"Hey, Buckwheat," came a tired voice from the living room.

Joshua walked in to find Davy crashed on the couch. “So what brings you here?”

“The car died and left me stranded,” mumbled Davy.

“That sucks. What happened to it?” Joshua asked.

“Oh, that crummy transmission gave out.”

“I'm sorry to hear that. So did your Dad send it to that great soup can factory in the sky?”

“It never made it home, so I did the next best thing.”

Joshua scratched his head. “What did you do?”

“I abandoned that stupid piece of junk in a no-parking zone and had to walk all the way here. And now I don't feel so good.”

“Maybe it was something you ate?” Joshua hinted, referring to the ice cream.

Davy got up from the couch. “Nah, but I think my stomach is broken.”

"Well, come on," replied Joshua. "I'll give you a ride home. Tomorrow will be a better day."

"No it won't," said Davy as he trudged toward the kitchen door. "I have a test in Psychology tomorrow."

* * *

Karen wasn't too surprised to see Joshua's car pull up in the driveway. That usually meant that Davy's car had broken down. On the other hand, if it was Davy's car in the driveway, it usually meant that Joshua's car broke down. But she was surprised at what she *didn't* see when she went out to the car.

"Where's Davy?" she asked as she got in the front seat. "Isn't he going to school this morning?"

"His Mom called me this morning. He was sick in bed."

Karen buckled her seatbelt. "Is he really sick, or is he just trying to get out of that Psychology test?"

Joshua backed out of the driveway. "No, I think he was really sick. He was crashed on the couch when I got home last night, and he didn't look very well. So he'll be missing Psychology today."

"On the other hand, I'm sure Mr. Fredericks won't be missing Davy in his class today," Karen said.

Joshua agreed. "Yeah, I heard that Mr. Fredericks is getting a little edgy these days."

7

Karen and Joshua thought they should visit Davy, so they stopped by his house after school. They pulled up by the garage where Davy's father ran his repair shop and salvage business. They popped inside the garage to say hello. They found him under the hood of a car.

"Hi, Mr. Odell!" said Joshua.

Hiram Odell glanced up. "Oh, hello! Say, hand me that wrench, would you?"

Karen picked it up and held it out to him. “How's Davy doing?” she asked.

“Hrrmph!” Hiram grunted. “He's been driving everyone nuts,” he replied as he took the wrench.

“So he's feeling better?” asked Joshua.

“Yeah...that bug he had didn't last very long. It started to wear off around noon. See if you can do something with him, would you?”

They agreed to try and headed up to the house. As soon as they walked in, they were greeted with the friendly barking of Hoover, the Odell's dog. Their cat, Go Away, rubbed up against Karen's leg the way he always did when he wanted some attention. She picked him up as Mollie called to them from the kitchen, “Hello! How are you two doing?”

“Pretty good,” Joshua replied as they made their way into the kitchen.

He opened a cupboard and pulled out a doggy treat for Hoover, who immediately sat up and begged. Joshua held it up for Hoover to see before tossing it in his direction. Hoover caught it mid-air, then settled down to munch on it. Go Away made himself comfortable in Karen's arms.

“How is Davy doing?” Karen asked.

“Oh, he'll be fine,” Mollie replied as she continued preparing dinner “He was feeling pretty bad this morning, but he's been driving everyone up the wall this afternoon. He's resting in front of the television at the moment. Try to do something with him, would you?”

They said they would try and went into the living room. Davy was stretched out across the living room sofa with a blanket over him, watching cartoons.

Karen was about to greet him, then paused to look at the television. She cocked her head sideways and asked, “Why did you prop the tv up on its side?”

“So I can watch cartoons laying down,” Davy said tiredly.

“I never would have thought of that,” said Joshua to Karen.

Go Away hopped out of Karen’s arms and onto the back of the couch.

“It takes an uncommon mind to think of these things,” quipped Davy.

Karen reached over and gave Davy's long blonde ponytail a gentle tug. “I'll grant you that one. So how are you feeling?”

“Better,” he said with a sigh. “Mom says I have to go to school tomorrow.”

“Feeling better enough for school?” asked Joshua.

“Not really, but Yvette got mad when I tried to use her bra as a double-barreled slingshot, then Mom got mad at me for it, then Dad found out and got mad at me for it, too. Then they took a vote and decided to let the school deal with me instead.”

“Outvoted three-to-one, huh?” said Karen.

“It was a rigged election. Wait until the ACLU gets wind of this one,” said Davy.

“So you want me to pick you up tomorrow?” asked Joshua.

“Sure,” Davy said. “But only if you promise not to take me to school.”

8

Joshua was eating dinner with his parents when he heard a familiar door slam shut. They looked up to see Davy walk in, armed with a gallon of orange juice. He walked in and sat down at the table, chugging the orange juice.

"Gee, Davy, why don't you make yourself at home?" asked Joshua's father in a rather sarcastic tone.

"Oh, no thanks," replied Davy. "I'm not very hungry."

“That's unusual,” said Joshua's mother. “Aren't you feeling well?”

Davy took another swig of juice. “I stayed home from school yesterday. I'm feeling better today. Good enough for Mom to kick me out of the house and make me go to school.”

He drank some more juice, then remarked, “What a rotten week this has been.”

“Why, what happened?” asked Joshua's mother.

“Well, first my car died and left me stranded. Then I got sick. Then Mom found out about my subscription to Nude Volleyball Magazine and cancelled it. Now, to top it all off, I have to make up the Psychology test I missed AND give my homework assignment as an oral presentation. I just can't win.”

“What's wrong with that?” asked Joshua. “You knew you would have to take it. Aren't you ready for it? Where's your textbook?”

“It's in my locker, and besides, that's not the point,” said Davy. “Fredericks said I could only take it at his house tonight... something about keeping an eye on me and fewer distractions and stuff. That's going to be worse than death!"

"Well, at least he was gracious enough to let you make it up," replied Joshua's father.

Davy took another swig of juice while contemplating this. "I can make up lots of things, but he usually doesn't like it."

Joshua's father gave a disapproving sigh. "That's putting it mildly, to say the least."

"Cheer up, Batman," Joshua chimed in. "It'll be all done and over with before you know it, then you can move on to other things."

"I wish I could just move."

"I wish you could just move, too," quipped Joshua's father.

Davy got up, bumping the table and rattling everything on it in the process. "Speaking of which, I have to get moving."

He trudged into the kitchen, tossed the empty juice container into the refrigerator, then hollered,

“Oh, and next time, buy the other kind of orange juice! I don't like the one with the floaties in it.”

9

Joshua's mother hung up the phone. "Joshua, that was Davy.. He said he would swing by to pick you up for school this morning."

"Thanks, Mom."

"So how do you suppose Davy did with his make-up test last night?"

Joshua busied himself loading his backpack, laughing a bit at her question. "Oh, knowing Davy he probably made the most of it."

"Is that good or bad?" she asked.

"Sometimes I don't want to know, but I—" He was interrupted by a horn honking from the driveway. "Oops, he's here already! Gotta run, Mom! Bye!" And with that, he slung his backpack over his shoulder and headed out the door.

Joshua started to hustle down the driveway, then slowed down as he saw Davy's latest ride. The car had no front-end sheet metal, doors, or trunk lid. It rode on four space-saver tires. He couldn't help but laugh when Davy called out, "Look, I got me a brand-new Mustang! Isn't it great?"

Joshua tossed his backpack in the back seat, then climbed in the front and fastened his seatbelt. "What happened to this one?"

Davy stepped on the clutch and started the car. "Oh, it's a recovered theft. They only got as far as swiping the wheels and body panels off before they got busted. Dad brought it home late last night and stuck it in the garage until they recover everything to put it back together."

"Does your Dad know about this?"

Davy put the car in first and eased out the clutch. "No." He banged off second gear, adding, "It's really easy to smoke off those little space saver spares! Doesn't corner very well, though."

It was a quick ride to Karen's house. Karen had the same reaction to the car that Joshua had. "At least I get to ride in a new Mustang!" she said.

After she got settled in the back seat, she asked, "So how did your test at Mr. Fredericks house go last night?"

"Oh, yeah!" exclaimed Joshua. "I almost forgot about that. Was it hard?"

"Not really, but it provided an interesting opportunity."

There was a moment of silence as Karen and Joshua pondered this. "What do you mean by that?" asked Karen rather hesitantly.

Davy shifted gears. "Well, when I got there, he had me sit in the living room to take the test. He sat across the room correcting papers while his wife sat next to him knitting something. He told me I had thirty minutes."

"So did you finish it?" asked Joshua.

Davy glanced over at Joshua. "Oh, sure. I breezed through it in ten minutes."

"See? I told you it wouldn't be so bad. And you even finished early!" said Joshua.

"Not really," Davy replied. "I still had twenty-five minutes."

"Wait...if you had thirty minutes and used ten, how do you end up with twenty-five?" asked Joshua.

Davy brought the car to a stop at an intersection and looked both ways before crossing. "They both dozed off, so I went around the house and set all their clocks back five minutes."

"Hence the 'opportunity,'" said Joshua, nodding.

"I swapped the locks between the front and back doors, too," he added.

"You did all that in twenty-five minutes?" asked Karen.

"Twenty, actually," replied Davy offhandedly. "All that work made me hungry, so I found some apple pie in the fridge that I couldn't pass up."

Joshua and Karen said nothing, so Davy continued. "After I ate, I sat down and hollered that I was done. Boy, that sure got their attention! I gave Fredericks my test and thanked him for letting me make it up, then I went home."

10

"So your Dad came for the Mustang, huh?" said Karen as they walked home from school.

"Yeah," replied Davy. "He was pretty mad about it, too. What a sorehead. How was I supposed to know that it was being held as evidence? These things wouldn't happen if he would tell me about them."

"How about Psychology? How did that go?" asked Joshua.

"Not so good. Fredericks didn't like my presentation."

"Why, what was wrong with it?" asked Karen.

Davy stopped to pick up a stick from the side of the street and began fiddling with it. "Well, we had to pick a product or service and discuss how they use advertising to influence the consumer's decision to buy it."

"So what was yours?" asked Joshua.

Davy screamed, "AAAUUUUUGH!
Insurance. Oatmeal went down the ductwork? Abducted by space aliens? Government steal everything you have? When disaster strikes, just remember AAAUUUUUGH! Insurance."

Joshua thought for a moment. "So you're the one I heard screaming earlier today."

Davy beamed. "Yeah, I'm told I was heard clear down in the auditorium."

"Geez, Davy," said Karen. "What did Fredericks think of that?"

Davy just shrugged. "Not much. He was running late this morning for some reason and looked a little frazzled, so he wasn't in a very good mood. He told me I had until Monday to come up with something a little more legitimate."

* * *

Joshua was so absorbed in his studies that he almost didn't hear the phone ring. He brought his textbook with him as he absentmindedly picked up the phone. "Hello?"

"Hey, Joshua, it's me, Davy!"

"What's up, Davy?"

"I need a ride. Can you come get me?"

Joshua set his textbook down. "Uh, sure... Where are you?"

"I'm at the funeral home!" Davy announced triumphantly.

Joshua was mildly shocked to hear this. "The funeral home? What happened? Is everything okay?"

"Oh, sure," came the offhanded reply. "I'll tell you all about it when you get here. Besides, it was nobody we know. Bye!"

Ten minutes later, Joshua pulled up in front of the funeral home. Davy was sitting on the front steps, reading a newspaper. He jumped up and plopped himself into the passenger seat before slamming the door shut.

"Thanks for the lift, Buckwheat."

"So what brings you here?" asked Joshua as he pulled onto the street.

"Dad serviced one of their hearses. They didn't have time to come get it, so he had me drive it over here. What a neat ride!"

"A hearse?"

"Yeah!" said Davy. "It does great burnouts. Pretty good stereo system, too. And look what I found!" he added, holding up the paper he was reading.

Joshua glanced over at what Davy had. "A news publication for funeral homes and cemeteries?"

"Yeah! This is great! Look at all the cool stuff they have in their classified section. Here's a marketing guide for funeral directors...used hearses for sale...a cremation service that you can like on Facebook or view on YouTube..."

Then he started to laugh hysterically. “Hey, look, here's a service for morbidly obese decedents! Here's one with a hot chick posing with some urns And this one is modeling next to a casket.

“Wow, check this out! If your loved one kicks off in some other country, you can mail him home in a nifty cardboard box! And here's another one with a guy floating around a pool in a...cremation tray?” Davy really cracked up at that one.

“Well,” said Joshua, “I suppose every business has to have some form of advertising.”

Davy continued to peruse the paper excitedly. “Oooh, they even get to have funeral directors conventions! Look, here's a picture of them dancing the conga. Boy, get a few drinks in them, and there's no telling what they'll do.”

“Well,” said Joshua, “even funeral directors have to have fun.”

“Yeah," agreed Davy. “They sure know how to put the fun in funeral! I wonder if any of them had a fling in the back of a hearse? I should get me one of those! I want mine to be orange.”

"So what are you doing with that catalog anyways?" asked Joshua, trying to change the subject.

"Well, when I dropped off the hearse, I was in the office and saw this. I snagged it on the way out. I'm going to use this to make up the Psychology assignment that Fredricks didn't like." Then he pulled out his notebook. "Oh, that reminds me," he added as he scribbled furiously.

Joshua was glad when they finally arrived at Davy's house so he wouldn't have to hear any more of it. They hopped out of the car and walked into the house, Davy talking at random about items in the paper. They went into the kitchen, where Davy's sister, Yvette, was making a large batch of fruit salad.

"Hi, Joshua!" Yvette was always happy to see him. "Would you like some fruit salad?"

"Hi Yvette! Yes, please."

Davy rolled up his paper and bopped Joshua over the head. "What's wrong with you? Don't be friendly with the enemy!"

Yvette responded to this by giving Davy a kick in the shin. “Hey, don't hit him!” When she turned around, Davy rolled up a towel and whipped her on the butt.

“Don't you tell me who I can and can't hit. Boy, if I had known I would end up with a sister like you, I would have been born first.”

“Oh yeah?” she scoffed. “If I had known I would end up with a kid brother like you, I would have made sure you were NEVER born.”

Yvette set a bowl of fruit salad down in front of Joshua and gave him a smile. “Here you are, Joshua. Ejoy!”

Davy looked over and scowled. “Hey, you lazy wench, where's mine? Gimme some fruit salad!”

Yvette scoffed at him. “Oh, you want some too, do you?”

“Yeah,” Davy shot back as he sat down. “Rustle up some grub right now.” Then he turned to Joshua and commented, “Good help is SO hard to find these days.”

“Oh, yeah?” retorted Yvette. “Fine. Here, Davy, you can have some fruit salad. In fact, you can have ALL the fruit salad you want!" she yelled, dumping the entire bowl on his head.

Davy shot up out of his chair screaming bloody murder. Yvette shrieked and bolted from the kitchen with Davy hot on her heels. Joshua said nothing. He simply picked up a magazine to read while Davy and Yvette tore around the house whooping and hollering at each other. Hoover and Go Away scurried in to take advantage of their unexpected bounty on the floor.

11

Joshua and Karen were sitting in the kitchen when Karen's mother walked in with a handful of mail. She puzzled over one piece before speaking. “There's a large envelope in your name, Joshua.”

Joshua looked up at the envelope that was being held towards him. “For me? That's weird. Why would I get mail at your house?”

Karen made a helpless gesture. “Are you trying to hide something from your parents?”

Joshua scratched his head. “No, I don't have any secrets...”

Just then, Davy walked in and saw the envelope. “Hey, it came!” he exclaimed.

Karen turned around. “What?”

Davy took the envelope from Mrs. Rodman's hand. “My new subscription to Nude Volleyball Magazine!”

“Wait a minute,” said Karen. “Why are you sending your mail to my house in his name?”

“So Mom doesn't find out. I think the mailman tipped her off. He doesn't like me.”

Mrs. Rodman spoke up. “I wish you had at least asked first.”

“Questions I know the answers to don't need to be asked!” replied Davy.

Joshua just shook his head. “I know better than to ask that one...”

Davy just gave him a silly look and peeked inside the envelope. “Oooh, the semi-finals issue! I'll save this one for later.”

Mrs. Rodman looked at Joshua. "Where does he find this stuff?"

"I don't know. I thought he was making it up."

Mrs. Rodman just shook her head and walked away.

"Hey Batman, how did your report about the funeral industry go?" Karen asked Davy.

Davy pulled out a chair and plopped himself down in it. "Oh, it was okay," he replied as he opened his notebook and scribbled a few things.

"Describe 'okay,'" said Joshua.

"Well, I gave the report, but most people thought it was too weird. Mr. Fredericks didn't think too highly of it, either."

"So what happened?" asked Karen.

"He told me that I really should put more effort into my assignments. I told him he already had one foot in the grave, so this was for his benefit." Noting the blank stares on Joshua and Karen's faces, he added, "I noticed he really quaffs down those meds these days, too. Must be for that weird twitch he developed."

* * *

"Did you get everything your Mom asked for?" asked Joshua.

Davy looked at the shopping list. "I think so. Oh, and grab a bag of those mini-marshmallows too. I'm hungry."

"That's not food. How about some apples instead?"

Davy blanched. "I don't want applies. Those aren't good food. I want something that's bad for me!"

Joshua took a bag off the shelf and tossed it into the shopping cart. "Grocery shopping always makes you hungry, doesn't it?"

"I'm in a big building full of food. Who wouldn't be hungry?"

Joshua and Davy made their way to the checkout to pay for the groceries. They each took a bag and headed out the door. Davy eyed the marshmallows that were poking out of Joshua's bags. "Hey Buckwheat, I'll trade bags with you."

"Forget it, Batman. You'll have to wait until we get to the car," Joshua chided as they stepped out to the sidewalk and made their way up the street.

"Yeah, well—hey, look! Isn't that Fredericks's car?" said Davy, eyeing the car parked up the street.

"Sure looks like it. Why?"

"I only know one man who drives something that boring. Quick, peek in the barbershop window. See if he's in there."

Joshua took a quick glance as they walked by. "Yeah, looks like he's just getting in the chair."

"Great! Here, hold these a minute," said Davy, shoving his bag into Joshua's arms.

Joshua struggled with the extra bag to regain his balance and grip. He looked up to see Davy reach under the bumper and produce a spare key, then hop into Mr. Fredericks car and start it up. He put on the turn signal, then carefully pulled out of the parking space and moved to the other side of the street. Joshua watched as Davy got out of the car, dropped some change in the parking meter, then returned the key before crossing the street to reclaim the bag of groceries.

Joshua sighed. “Well, let's get going so we don't keep your mom waiting.”

“No, not just yet! Let's sit in the car for a few minutes, I want to see how this turns out.”

Seeing the look on Joshua's face, he said, “I'll share my marshmallows with you.”

12

Davy was busy scribbling in his notebook when Joshua and Karen sat down across from him at the cafeteria table.

"You've been writing a lot lately, Davy," said Karen. "Care to share some of it with us?"

"Not yet," replied Davy. "It's still top-secret."

"Psychology?" asked Joshua.

"Yep," said Davy as he closed the notebook.

“So how is it going?” asked Joshua.

“I'm not sure,” said Davy, scratching his head. “I noticed he's kind of moody these days, so it's hard to figure him out. Like today, for example.”

“Why, what happened today?” asked Karen.

Davy sighed thoughtfully. “Well...there was a pretty good discussion going about the psychology behind religion versus science. Then people started arguing about whether we evolved from apes or started from scratch, and finally someone asked me what I thought.”

“I want to hear this,” said Joshua to Karen. “This should be really good.”

“Well, it works like this. See, when God was a kid, he was throwing rocks. His mom told him to knock it off before he hit something. Then he let one fly, and it hit the earth and wiped out all the dinosaurs. Lucky for him, his mom wasn't home. So he tried to fix it before she came back. He managed to glue everything back together again, sort of, but he wasn't very good at making dinosaurs. They turned out like people and animals, and that's how we got here.”

Joshua and Karen looked at each other, then at Davy. Noticing the perplexed looks on their faces, he added, “And his mom never found out, either.”

Joshua scratched his head. “Like how your mother's electric beater ended up at the bottom of the pond?”

Davy thought a moment. “Sort of. It was more like the time I used Dad's electric razor on a coconut. He never found out about that one, remember?”

“So what did Fredericks think?” asked Karen.

Davy just shrugged. “I don't think he was paying attention. He was too busy mixing his meds.”

* * *

Davy was in the back seat of the car, scribbling away in his notebook. Joshua sat in the driver’s seat, going through some notes. They were waiting for Karen after school. It wasn't long before she came running out the door and hopped inside the car.

“Hey, guess what happened?” she said excitedly.

“What?” replied Davy, barely glancing up from his notebook.

"Mr. Fredericks quit today!" she exclaimed.

"What? Really? When did this happen?" asked Joshua.

"Just a few minutes ago. I brought some papers down to the office, and he was in there ranting and raving. Said he couldn't take it any longer."

"Why, what happened?" said Joshua.

"I only heard a little bit. Something about a kid driving him crazy, and... and..." her voice trailed off as a thought crossed her mind. She looked at Joshua, who had arrived at a similar conclusion.

They slowly looked back at Davy, who had stopped writing in his notebook and closed it before tossing it aside. "Oh well, at least I proved my theory," he sighed.

"What theory is that?" asked Joshua rather hesitantly.

"Well," he started, pausing to open a bag of cheese puffs. "When we started the class, we had to observe how people react in certain situations, so I decided to conduct an experiment. I picked a subject—I named him Mr. X—

and took notes on how he dealt with unexpected disruptions in his daily routine."

"Davy!" scolded Karen. "You've been messing with Mr. Fredericks to test a theory?"

"Yeah," replied Davy as he upended the bag into his mouth, spilling a few in his lap.

"And what did your theory prove?" asked Joshua.

Davy chewed and swallowed thoughtfully, then held up the bag in a toast. "You can't teach an old Fred new tricks!"

About The Author

Craig Merrow is a machinist for the United States Navy and enjoys writing, taking courses at the local college, early jazz, old radio shows, picking blueberries, and mountain biking. He is always busy with some new project, his latest being the design and construction of an off-grid solar home in Southern Maine.

About The Publisher

Story Shares is a nonprofit focused on supporting the millions of teens and adults who struggle with reading by creating a new shelf in the library specifically for them. The ever-growing collection features content that is compelling and culturally relevant for teens and adults, yet still readable at a range of lower reading levels.

Story Shares generates content by engaging deeply with writers, bringing together a community to create this new kind of book. With more intriguing and approachable stories to choose from, the teens and adults who have fallen behind are improving their skills and beginning to discover the joy of reading. For more information, visit storyshares.org.

Easy to Read. Hard to Put Down.

Made in the USA
Middletown, DE
20 January 2023